A Note from the Aut

Fishy Tales is based on a puppet show I wrote six years ago for Day of Puppetry. This annual celebration is hosted by the Phoenix Guild of Puppetry, the Great Arizona Puppet Theater, and Puppet Pie. It is a wonderful day full of puppet activities, from professional puppet shows to make-and-take puppets, puppet parades, and a puppet show performed by the children in attendance. All these activities provide an opportunity for children to show their puppetry skills for friends and family.

I wrote *Fishy Tales* as a way to involve as many children as possible in a production. Children ages three to twelve created fish, octopuses, and trash puppets. Using a blue bed sheet, we created an ocean. A narrator read the story, and the children performed with their handmade puppets. The show was a success, and I have used it at other events as well.

Working with children on this puppet show inspired me to write and illustrate *Fishy Tales* the book. Children have told me that the story is important to them. They are concerned about the future of the oceans. They want to be involved in solutions for saving our planet from climate change.

I would like to thank the Phoenix Guild of Puppetry, the Great Arizona Puppet Theater, and Puppet Pie for their promotion of storytelling and puppetry in the greater Phoenix area. They have truly made a difference in my life and the lives of countless children over the years.

I would also like to thank all of you who have supported me as I took this journey as an author and illustrator. I hope you will enjoy this book and share it with your friends and family.

Editor:
Elisabeth Rinaldi

Publisher:
We Are Puppeteers, LLC
Mesa, AZ
Website: wearepuppeteers.com

Paperback ISBN: 978-1-7341268-6-0
Hardback ISBN: 978-1-7341268-5-3

Library of Congress Control Number: 2021921435

Printer:
MyBookPrinter/360 Digital Books/Whitlock
Website: mybookprinter.com

We Are Puppeteers

Fishy Tales

Written and Illustrated by Vicki Riske

Edited by Elisabeth Rinaldi

copyright 2021

Once upon time there were six fish friends. Each one was a rainbow color: red, orange, yellow, green, blue, and purple.

The fish loved to swim, splash, and play in the ocean.
Their favorite game was Marco Polo.

"I'll be it," said Ruby, jumping up and down in the water.
He covered his eyes with a rainbow mask and shouted, "Marco!"

"Polo!" shouted the other fish as they quickly swam away from Ruby.

The fish shouted back and forth, "Marco!" "Polo!" "Marco!" "Polo!" "Marco!" "Polo!" All the time laughing and splashing in the water.

Ruby was about to tag Violet when they heard a loud cry.
"Help! Help! Help!"

The fish stopped to listen, except Ruby.
He crashed right into Violet. SPLAT!

"You're it," said Ruby. "No, I am not it! said Violet. "I had to stop, because we heard a cry for help."

The cries for help grew louder. "HELP! ME!"

The fish swam quickly toward the cries for help.

Suddenly, they saw a large island of trash floating toward them.

The fast swimming fish could not stop and crashed into the trash.
SPLAT! SPLAT! SPLAT! SPLAT! SPLAT! and SPLAT!

"Ouch! Ouch!" screamed Amber. "Where did all this trash come from?"
"I don't know," said Jade, trying to untangle herself from the trash.

"The cries for help are coming from the trash," said Jade.
"Maybe someone is buried under the trash."

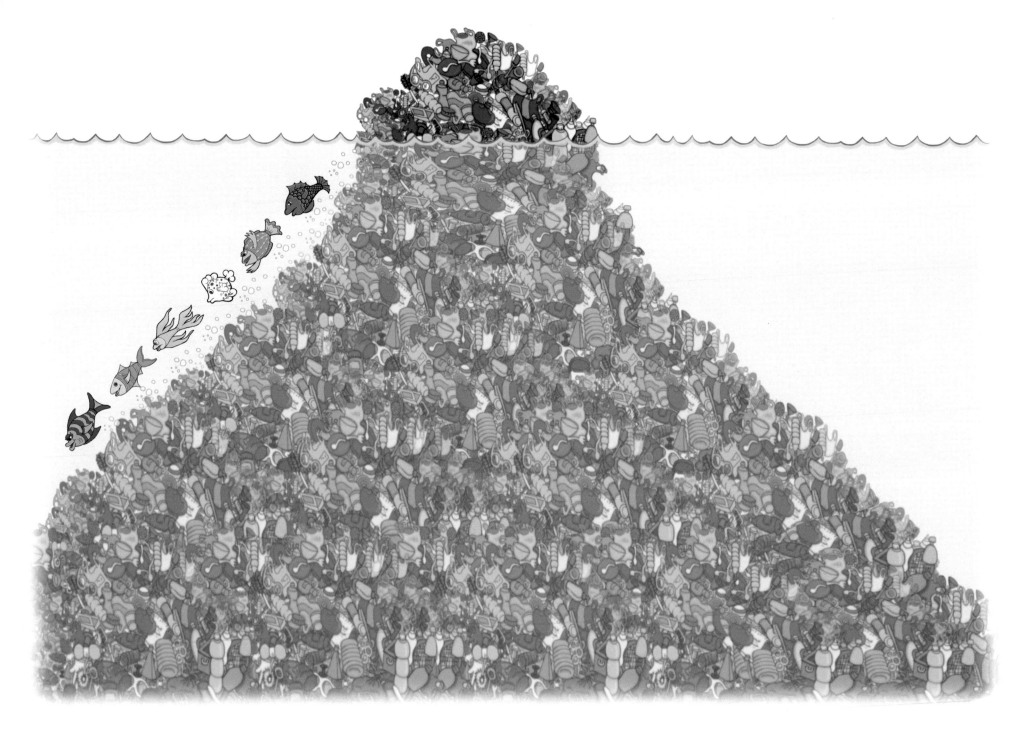

The fish tried to swim under the island, but the trash went too deep.

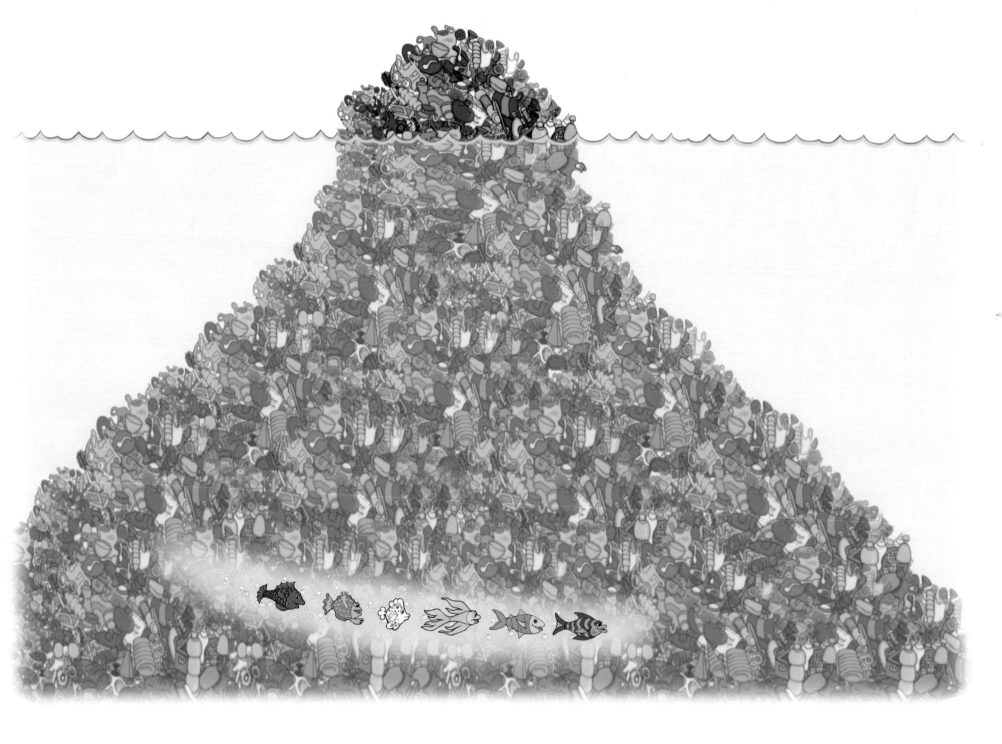

The fish tried to swim around the island, but the trash was too wide.

So the fish went back to the top of the island and started digging.
The trash went flying everywhere.

Soon they found one arm, then two, then three, four, five, six, seven, eight arms.

The fish pulled more trash away, and Olivia Octopus popped out.

"It's an octopus!" cried the fish.

"Please come closer so I can hug each one of you," said Olivia.

"No! You will eat us!" cried all the fish.

"I won't eat you. I want to thank you for saving me!" said Olivia.

"I want to be your friend forever."

"Look at my babies," said Olivia as her six babies crawled out of the trash.

"They are so cute," said Goldie.

"But they need clean water to live.
Plastic trash is hurting them." said Olivia.

"Plastic trash is a danger for all of us," said Goldie.

"What can we do to get rid of this trash island?" asked Violet.

"We need people to help clean up the ocean," said Olivia.

Jade and Amber found a ship named *Kindness* and asked the people on the ship for help.

The people agreed to help and followed the fish to the trash island.

People called their friends and neighbors and asked them
to help remove the trash from trash island.

And soon people came from all over the world.
They worked together to clean up the trash.

"Where are they taking the plastic trash?" asked Blueberry.

"The trash is going to recycling centers all over the world. Scientists, grandparents, parents, and children are all working on new ideas to reuse plastic trash and keep it out of our oceans," explained Olivia.

"Let's all work together to keep our oceans clean," said Olivia.
"So we can all live happily ever after!" shouted everyone.